TRIPS TO THE EDGE

TALES *of the* UNEXPECTED

Diane Wing

Modern History Press

Library of Congress Cataloging-in-Publication Data

Wing, Diane, 1959-
  [Short stories.]
  Trips to the edge : tales of the unexpected / by Diane Wing.
      pages cm
  ISBN 978-1-61599-262-1 (pbk. : alk. paper) -- ISBN 978-1-61599-263-8 (ebook)
  1. Paranormal fiction, American. I. Title.
  PS3623.I652A6 2015
  813'.6--dc23
                                    2014045136

Published by Modern History Press
an imprint of
Loving Healing Press
5145 Pontiac Trail
Ann Arbor, MI 48105

www.ModernHistoryPress.com
info@ModernHistoryPress.com
Tollfree 888-761-6268

Distributed by Ingram Book Group (USA/CAN), Bertram's Books (UK/EU)

Contents

Another Walk in the Park

It was just another walk in the park. A gentle summer breeze blowing, rustling the dense leaves on the trees. The occasional chipmunk suddenly bounding across my path and disappearing on the other side. Butterflies flew alongside, guiding my journey. I followed the same path I had countless times before, knowing what was around the next bend, changes only made by the seasons.

The big old oak ahead was mostly dead; yet refused to go quietly. Its twisted trunk, bulging bark, and thick, broken branches gave it an angry, evil countenance and dual personality when viewed from the other side, where its skin was smoother and new branches sprouted from the top of the broken trunk. There was a large opening at the base that I could fit inside easily to experience the spooky tree from its core, yet never did. It seemed an invasion to enter through this spirit portal. Out of respect, I looked in, but maintained our separateness.

Teenaged black walnut trees danced in a circle to mark the boundary of a large grove, a sacred space that seemed to have an energy all its own. The grass grew thick, awaiting park employee intervention to trim it back. Just to the left, a four-foot high, rough-hewn headstone proclaimed that this was the site of the Winterton Mansion, circa 1785. There seemed to be an energetic residue left from the mansion, accompanied by a sense of fore-boding. I had walked up to the stone many times, yet felt an invisible barrier that prevented me from moving past it and into the walnut grove.

A friend of mine was with me on one of my woodland walks and as we stood before the headstone, she commented that the house does not like attention drawn to it and prefers that visitors disregard its presence. The story goes that the house burned down and that the area is haunted. Some park visitors have smelled smoke and heard screams. My visits had, up to this point, been uneventful, having established good rapport with the trees and nature spirits in the area. Yet there was always an underlying sense of an alternate dimension, of layers waiting to be discovered, and of the distant past wanting to be remembered, waiting to be explored.

While usually approaching with great respect and reverence, this time felt different. It was as though the barrier was thinner, and the area was no longer off-limits. My feet were on the dirt path, but the grove beckoned me to visit, to experience, to cross into another time, another place. All six senses were on alert, prickling from past encounters with the area, teetering between honoring its solitude and an intense curiosity drawing me closer. Something tickled my ankle, and I realized I was standing in the overgrown grass halfway between the path and the headstone.

The headstone glared at me in silence, daring me to come forward, to break the seal and the unspoken agreement we had to remain apart. I telepathically assured this sacred space that I meant no harm and asked if I was being invited in. The answer flitted through my mind. I was to proceed at my own risk. Nothing would prevent me from being drawn into another world, if I chose to move forward. My choice, my responsibility. I became intensely aware of the sounds of creatures and leaves and wind. A butterfly came close to my face and fluttered off, as though reminding me that transformation was inevitable, warning me that once I took the next step, there was no turning back and nothing would be the same again.

Could I pass up the chance to explore an otherworldly realm? With all of my fantastical literary journeys, was I willing to engage in the unknown for real? Another step and the familiar background music of nature died, replaced by a sinister hush, as though the world, as I knew it, no longer existed. Now I was in the kingdom of yesteryear, a time forgotten and supposedly put to rest. Yet there was no rest for this grove, this tragic site that held within it the pain of those who perished in the fire. Wondering if I could turn back and reenter my own world, I surprised myself and committed to this journey by taking another step forward.

I found myself in a field surrounded by shrubs. The ancient oak and black walnut trees did not exist, for I was in a time before their planting. It was dusk, and fireflies were beginning to twinkle. Something shimmered a short distance away. The air felt dense as I cautiously approached the apparition. It began to solidify, first with an outline, and then filling itself in, as though an invisible child sat filling in the lines of a coloring book.

What emerged was a massive farmhouse, painted a muted taupe color with deeper brown-gray trim. Ornamental posts held up the wraparound front porch. Rocking chairs sat waiting to accommodate the home's inhabitants.

Despite its solid appearance, I questioned if my mind had conjured it using all the speculations and imaginings of the house that occupied the tranquil grove my many walks past. A sizzling wave of electricity washed over me, making my skin prickle. I took a step back to see if I could get out of the electromagnetic field and rubbed my arms to get the hair to lay flat.

I could not take my eyes off the house as the pulsing energy continued to bombard my head and chest. With each beat, the house seemed to pixilate, as when a television set goes on the fritz. The sound of electricity running through power lines accompanied the throbbing—the house and energy in perfect synchronicity as it hit me over and over. My hands began to numb, and I realized my legs were shaking. The constant hum of the energy tormented me, and I wished it would stop. My nerves jangled from the barrage of impulses. I took several steps backward and finally disengaged from the energy.

Eyes were on me, and my eyes rose to the center window on the second floor. A pale man watched as I disentangled myself from the force field. He wore a sinister, satisfied grin, and I understood that it was his intention to cause discomfort. My reaction had pleased and amused him. My desire to return to my own time overwhelmed me, and I ran the way I had come, hoping to go through the barrier once again.

When I found myself beyond the entry border and was almost run over by a horse-drawn carriage, a sinking feeling took over my body, and I fell to my knees. The driver did not even acknowledge me, as though I did not exist in his world. By all rights, I should not have. But the grass I lay upon felt real enough. The anomaly crushed all sense of logic and reason. The house had let me in, but would not allow my return… just yet. There was something that beckoned me back. The man in the window was not finished with me.

My chest heaved, and it was difficult to catch my breath as panic at being forever trapped in this time warp overcame me. I knew instinctively that the longer I delayed returning to the phantom dwelling, the more extended my stay would be. Heart pounding, I pushed myself up and brushed off my hands. Looking up, I saw the face was no longer in the window.

With a deep sigh of resignation, I built up the courage to take a step toward the spectral house. The air around me pulsed in waves as I moved slowly toward the well-cared-for farmhouse. If it had existed in my own time and dimension, I would have been excited to visit the historic property and explore its secrets. Yet, having stepped through the invisible portal and into another plane of existence brought a foreboding that begged caution.

I stood before the front porch, the house completely solid, and gazed at rocking chairs that invited me to sit while I contemplated the dilemma of entering the house. The first step creaked as I stepped onto it; the second step was firm underfoot and maintained its silence. Two more stairs, and I was on the porch, staring at the front door. My guts shook at the thought of entering, so I gave myself respite in one of the rockers. It was comfortable but not comforting as I tried to rock my way into a state of relaxation.

Back and forth, gently rocking, daring not to think, the old boards of the porch creaked under the movement. I wanted so desperately to be back in the park on the side of the energy field that held my life. Daring to close my eyes for a moment, my ears perked up at the sound of the front door whining as it slowly opened. I leapt up from the chair to face whatever was about to emerge, but nothing came forth. I took small steps to glance into the darkness beyond the threshold, preparing for the worst.

Light did not pierce the shadows within the gaping doorway. I crept closer and could see dust swirling in the faint light coming through the back door window. A straight, steep staircase to my right led to the second floor. Whatever had opened the door was hiding, and I feared it would jump out and attack with ferocity. Heart pounding as my thoughts continued to worsen, I forced myself forward. *Would it grab me? Was the pale man in the window waiting, armed with a knife or a gun, poised to harm me at the first opportunity?*

Silence greeted me at the door. No movement. A dank smell of wet, burned timber wafted toward me. The quiet held me hostage; reluctance stripped me of all courage, as I waited for something to happen. So unnerving was the hush that I called out a meek and questioning *hello*. Was I crazy to hasten the inevitable or just tired of being frightened by the unknown? At least if something emerged, I could deal with it.

No response. I called out again, a bit more boldly this time, and finally received an answer.

"It's about time you grew a pair instead of sounding like a wimp."

The voice came from the top of the stairs. I gazed up to see a dark silhouette, his arm holding the newel post. I took a step closer. Dim light shone from the window at the top of the stairs and his form came into focus. It was the pale man I had seen in the upper window.

"Excuse me?"

"You heard me. Can't be here unless you have balls."

He sounded matter-of-fact, as though everyone knows that to cross into another dimension there must be a certain amount of courage.

"I'm not sure how I got here," I stammered.

"Well now, your curiosity dragged you in here. You've been past this place so many times I've lost count. Was wondering when you were finally going to break through."

The thought that he had been watching me each time I walked through the park made me shiver.

"How do I get back?"

"You don't."

"What?"

"You're not finished what you need to do here."

"And what exactly is that?" My voice reflected my thinning patience.

"Come on in, and I'll give you the tour."

All I wanted was to go home, but it sounded like that was not going to happen until I complied with his instructions. Rudeness on my part was not going to help my cause. I gingerly stepped across the threshold. My host was now halfway down the staircase. He wore a plaid shirt, overalls, and work boots. He looked to be in his early forties. His common appearance belied the hypnotic energy that radiated from him. I tried to look away, but his eyes held me in place.

He waved his hand toward the sparsely furnished living room. The austere handmade wood furniture lacked cushions to make guests feel welcome. It smacked of the desire for the briefest of visits by outsiders. A shadow, the shape of a woman wearing the full skirts of the time, moved across the wall and disappeared through a doorway. The man seemed not to notice.

"What is your name, sir?" I asked, hoping for a clue as to what was going on.

He turned toward me, a glimmer of secrets in his eyes.

"Jasper Winterton. This has been my home for centuries."

He offered no additional explanation and turned to continue the tour. Bewilderment set in. It was the name on the headstone. How was any of this possible?

Jasper moved through the doorway where the phantasm exited. I reluctantly followed, heart pounding, ears buzzing from the rush of blood. I had no desire to discover what happened to the apparition and hoped that it was not waiting for me.

The doorway led into the kitchen. The walls had smears of dark ash across them.

"This is where it started," Jasper said with anguish in his voice.

"Where what started?"

"The fire. Killed my wife and daughters. They didn't have a chance."

All I could do was nod in sympathy. I looked around. The walls and floors were solid enough. But the smell of wet, burned wood persisted, reflecting the tragic history of Jasper's home. He was tied to this place out of remorse.

"I'm so sorry to hear that."

"Not at all. It happened just as I planned... well, almost as planned," Jasper said matter-of-factly.

My eyes widened as I stared at this murderer.

"As you planned?" I stammered.

"Yep. The kids burned up in the fire, but my wife, Lola, got out before the smoke and flames got her. She took her own life later. Couldn't tolerate losing the girls."

"But you lost everything... your family, your home..."

"Those things weren't important to me. They were holding me back."

I rubbed my hands and noticed how cold they were. I silently prayed for protection. His casual attitude made my chest feel tight. I swallowed deeply and summoned my courage. This man didn't like wimps.

"So how come you're still here?"

"I'm required to stay here," he said.

"Required?"

"It was the price I paid for freedom many years ago. And I plan to have my freedom once again! Time for you to see the second floor."

My heart sank and my stomach quivered. There wasn't anything good waiting for me on the second floor.

"That's okay, I've seen enough. I think I'll just be on my way," I said as calmly as I was capable of.

"There's no hurry. You can see it now or you can see it tomorrow. Doesn't matter much to me."

"I won't be here tomorrow."

"What makes you think that? You're not going anywhere."

"I'm expected at home. They'll come looking for me."

"They can look all they want, but they won't find you. You're in my land now, son."

My head dropped. Fear, frustration, and sorrow mingled together and made my body start to shake.

"Now, now," said Jasper, "You need to get over it. Just accept it for what it is."

"And exactly what is it?" I hollered.

"Well that's what I've been trying to show you. Follow me."

Jasper turned and walked through the doorway, through the living room, and out into the hallway. He stood by the stairs waiting for me to follow. My legs refused to move, and the shaking made me feel unsteady. I gulped air and closed my eyes, trying to calm myself. The longer I resisted Jasper, the more I delayed leaving this place. I opened my eyes and saw the female shadow figure pointing toward the doorway. That was the motivation I needed to hurry out of the kitchen, run through the living room, and breathlessly join Jasper at the foot of the steps.

"She's quite persuasive, wouldn't you say?" Jasper chuckled. "C'mon up and meet the rest of the family."

He waved to me to follow as he trudged up the well-worn wooden stairs. His solid footfall landed on the center of each step where the finish showed wear; a creak sounding every so often. I grabbed the top of the newel post and treaded lightly behind him, watching the unfamiliar steps as I walked. Looking up, I saw him waiting at the top, arms crossed, tapping his foot. I picked up the pace a bit.

As I neared the top of the staircase, he walked to the left and down a dim hallway, then stood in front of a door. The shaking intensified again, and I worried that my legs would give out on me. I steadied myself against the wall. Jasper pushed open the door and light flowed into the space. He gestured for me to enter the room.

I slowly approached the doorway and became aware of the quick, sharp breaths I was taking. I peeked around the entry and saw twin beds, each with a female child sitting, and both quietly staring at each other. Their dresses were a dingy gray color, faces smeared with ash, ribbons adorning their messy hair, and eyes blank.

"These are my daughters, Megan and Polly." Jasper said with disdain.

They did not turn to acknowledge me; just stayed eerily still.

"They're much easier to deal with in this state." Jasper commented. "They won't give you too much trouble."

I looked at him, mouth gaping.

"What do they have to do with me?"

"You're their new caretaker."

"I don't think so."

"It'll give you a second chance, like I got."

"At what?"

"At safeguarding children. My wife, too, can't forget about her."

"What are you talking about?"

"I know you said it was an accident, but when you left your son in that hot box on wheels, you intended to kill him."

"In my car? That was an accident. He climbed in the back and fell asleep. I didn't know he was in there. Helen should have been watching him." I defended myself with the same line I used on the jury, but Jasper had nailed me, when the authorities couldn't.

"Come now, son, kids are a nuisance. You had better things to do than to deal with a kid and a woman who tricked you into marriage. Sins of the flesh will get you every time."

"She was pregnant. It was the right thing to do." I spouted my rehearsed objection. I had always resented Helen for lying to me about being on the pill; but how did Jasper know that?

"She couldn't bear the loss of her boy, so she took her own life. You succeeded, son."

I bit my lip and winced as he shoved the truth in my face. There was nothing I could say.

"Just so you know, you won't need anything to eat. You're in perpetual status."

"What the hell does that mean?" I shouted.

"It's the name They told me when I arrived. I think it means that it's a place between worlds, where nothing of earthly needs is required."

"So I'm supposed to stay here with you forever?"

My heart was in my throat and the adrenalin was pumping, telling me to run.

"Nowhere to run, son," Jasper read my mind. "You'll get used to it. Nice and quiet here. Nothing to worry about. I won't be around, but your wife and kid will be here shortly."

"What!"

"You won't need to pay much attention to 'em. My wife and kids will be here to entertain 'em."

I opened my mouth, but no words came out.

"Come across the way here, and I'll show you your room."

He led me to a bedroom at the front of the house. There was a small table and chair next to the window. It was where I first glimpsed him from outside.

"I find this spot to be where you can keep an eye on things outside." He pulled the chair out and nodded his head for me to sit. A leather-bound journal sat open on the table with a fountain pen resting in its open spine. "Writing can soothe the nerves and clear your head. They brought a fresh one for you."

I flipped through the lined pages. They were blank, waiting for me to put my thoughts on paper.

"I think it's supposed to help atone for your sins. Admit what you did, and you'll get a replacement sooner than later. It took me a good long time before I was willing to come to terms with my deed; but once I did, you showed up."

Jasper walked to the bedroom door and held the knob.

"Best of luck, son."

He closed the door gently behind him.

I sat, dumbfounded at the turn of events. It was an odd feeling, a knowing and on some level accepting that I was trapped here. I was not looking forward to spending eternity here, so I vowed to make peace with Them and with my transgressions as quickly as possible. I picked up the pen and began to write.

As I sit writing from my perch in the upper floor of the farmhouse, I can see the park visitors enjoying their woodland walk, glancing into the clearing, unaware of my presence as I await a visitor to take my place.

Dark Hollow Road

Emptiness consumed her since her brother, Mitch, had disappeared down Dark Hollow Road last month. He was not the first to go missing from this mysterious stretch of road that ran from the middle of town and straight into the deep forest. The trees went on for miles, and those who chose not to heed the warnings of those who had lost loved ones to the road were never seen again. Then again, it is possible that they simply refused to return to the town of Dark Hollow after being able to escape its unsettling silence filled with secrets better left unknown.

In a lifetime of living in Dark Hollow, torn between fascination and fear, Rachel did some safe investigating. Part of her wanted desperately to discover what went on in the dense forest and to see if there was an end to Dark Hollow Road. At first she consulted the Internet to see if MapQuest could give her a bird's eye view of the area. Neither MapQuest nor any of the other map websites acknowledged the existence of Dark Hollow Road. Neither the map view nor the satellite view gave her a glimpse of the path the road followed.

She tried Google World and pulled up a satellite image of the town of Dark Hollow. Selecting the hybrid view, she was able to see the roads she recognized, all except Dark Hollow Road. It showed a primary road in the middle of town called Main Street, which was accurate for that portion of the road. Then the road ended and turned into woods.

Rachel moved the image to see past the dense forest and looked for the road to come out the other side, but the trees grew over the road for miles. The next bit of street to emerge showed itself in Blakely, which was the next town over. She wished she knew someone there so she could find out if there were disappearances at their end of this curious road.

Looking out the window, she could see the sun shining on the treetops and wondered about the mysteries held within the forest. Rachel pulled on her Bucks County Community College sweatshirt and headed downstairs, past the living room, where her mother watched an endless stream of soap operas. Losing herself in the storylines of imaginary characters proved easier than dealing with the loss of her son. Rachel called to her saying she would be back soon, as she walked out the front door. Telling her she intended to venture to the edge of the woods on Dark Hollow Road would have caused a complete uproar.

It was only a short walk to where Mitch had driven his beat-up, blue Mustang into the darkness. Rachel could not understand why her brother would do that, knowing the stories of that road as well as anyone. In his 27 years living in this town, at least three of his friends had let curiosity get the best of them, and they ventured into the forbidden zone, never to return.

Standing in the last bit of sunlight before the trees blocked out its rays, Rachel peered into the shadows. The two police barriers painted with bright orange stripes and the words DANGER – DO NOT CROSS stenciled in black across the horizontal wood blockade had been moved aside, probably by a skeptical traveler feeling the warning did not apply to them. Rachel, too, stepped past the ineffective obstacle and stood at the boundary between the town and the unknown. There was a tangible weight to the air around her—a heaviness felt the moment she stepped beyond the barrier. The dead silence of the woods was unnerving—no bird chirped; no animal scurried; and no wind rustled the leaves.

With summer coming to an end, it was worrisome to think of longer nights when the darkness of the forest could gain strength and hold her brother closer like the inescapable gravity of a black hole. She called Mitch's name, hoping he would answer, but her voice was sucked into silence along with all the rest of the sounds of the forest. Then she tried yelling to him telepathically, desperate to connect with him. Nothing.

Daring to take a step closer, the tip of Rachel's sneaker went into the soft shadow. It felt cooler than the rest of her shoe, which still baked in sunlight. The other foot followed, plunging deeper into shadow than the first.

With her right hand, she tested the temperature of the darkness. She had read somewhere that when there is an apparition present, the temperature dropped. It was a bit cooler, but not the way she guessed it felt when a ghost was nearby. Rachel looked behind her, not sure what she expected to see, thinking of her mother and the complete breakdown she would have if Rachel did not return. The thought was not enough to stop her from plunging her entire body into the shade of the trees. She had to find Mitch. She could not bear to think of him hurt and alone with no hope of rescue and no attempts made to retrieve him.

He had always been there for her. Mitch was her best friend and she relied on him as her older brother to guide her through the uncertainty of the transition from late teens to young adulthood. They had a special relationship, able to know each other's thoughts and to communicate mind-to-mind when they did not want their mother to know what was going on. Rachel felt the preternatural bond with Mitch from the moment she was consciously aware as a child. She needed him in her life.

Standing in the shadowy coolness, she felt the expected relief from the heat of the sun, but nothing supernatural in the surroundings. The quiet that ordinarily would have brought a sense of peace was disrupted by the sense of foreboding that escalated with every step. Following the pull of the road, Rachel walked forward tentatively, knowing the danger, yet ignoring the mental alarms going off in her head. Thoughts of her mother happy again at Mitch's return and the gratitude toward Rachel for bringing him back overwhelmed her common sense. The longing to reunite with her brother gave her courage to continue deeper into the forest.

The green of the leaves and the brown bark peeking out from behind the dense foliage calmed her nerves. She could smell the decaying leaves on the forest floor mingled with the cleansing scent of pine. Intoxicated by the surroundings, she allowed herself to be led, no longer aware of her feet moving one after the other, the soft sound of her sneakers hitting pavement. Awareness was limited to her eyes and nose. If she had gone deaf, she would not know, for she heard no sound.

Looking behind her, the sunlight was overshadowed by the dense forest. Unsure of how long she had been walking, the sun might have set; yet ample light illuminated her path as she strode deeper and deeper into the woods. The paved road stayed beneath her feet. She wondered if the workers who built the road had run into problems with their coworkers disappearing. Her research had not turned up any mention of the road being constructed, as if it had simply appeared without human activity.

She experienced no fatigue, no hunger, and no question about continuing her journey to find Mitch. Up ahead, she saw a tall structure covered in ivy. It looked like it was made of stone, pillars stretching upward to fifteen feet. A strange glow emanated from its center, and Rachel could see that it was an archway. Its design reminded her of a Grecian temple.

Gazing through the gateway, Rachel saw waves of blue and white, pulsating then swirling together with hints of lavender. She scanned the woods that surrounded the archway. Behind it and to either side were simply more of the same woods she had passed on her way to this spot. Upon closer inspection, she saw the headlight of a car peeking out from under a tangle of vines. Unsure of what type of vine and unwilling to contract poison sumac, she found a stick and moved them aside, revealing a very dirty blue Ford Mustang—Mitch's car!

Her forehead glistened with sweat as she contemplated the next step on her journey through the portal. If she had brought a pen and paper, she could have written Mitch a note requesting he come out and see her, wrapped it around a rock, and then thrown it through the portal. She could still throw a rock through to see what happens. Looking around, she found one the size of her palm and two inches high, hefty enough to toss through the shimmering waves to test its effect. Standing about five feet from the doorway, she gently tossed the rock. The portal silently sucked the stone into its field with barely a ripple.

Taking another step closer, Rachel peered into the swirls of color, trying to catch a glimpse of movement, hoping to see Mitch walking on the other side. Standing in proximity to the opening made her head swim and her body restless. A tug on her body encouraged her to step even closer to the mesmerizing vortex. Her desire to shed the constraints of the world she knew brought forth thoughts of freeing herself as a snake sheds its skin.

Unaware of movement, she had inched closer to the portal, now standing only two feet away and being drawn closer. She was no longer moving of her own volition, but gliding toward the threshold. Her body relaxed as the concern for her mother melted away. Rachel closed her eyes and let out a sigh as her body slid gently through a soft, gel-like substance. She flowed in a state of flux with no notion to stop or go, as though drifting in a rowboat, letting the current take her along for the ride. A sense of wonder made her stomach flutter and her body tingle. She did not know where she was going and oddly, did not care.

The substance surrounding her began to feel lighter against her skin, and she was able to open her eyes. Her gaze fell on a glowing, light blue horizon that intensified into a deep, soothing Caribbean blue, swirled through with cloudlike fog. It was so peaceful, so warm.

Images of people bobbing in the mist came into focus, and they beckoned her to their gathering. She felt as though she were coming home and this was a reunion, being welcomed into their fold and bathing her with love and acceptance. She was eager to join them and searched among their smiling faces until her eyes fell on Mitch. His handsome face radiated joy at the sight of her, his arms outstretched, waiting to enfold her. Rachel glided toward him, willing herself to move faster to feel his embrace. In his arms, the hug completed her, her joy soaring at their reunion.

Their hands still joined, she stood back from him and looked around her. He smiled broadly as he watched her jaw drop and her breath catch. Next to them was a rock-strewn creek flowing with sparkling blue and purple water. Blue mountains dotted with green shrubs and ancient evergreens soared in the background punctuated by several large plants glowing orange and yellow against a pale blue sky. Her feet rested on pink marble steps flecked with gold.

Her eyes widened at the sight of flower beds filled with beautiful crystal flowers growing in a nest of emerald green leaves. A lush green meadow sprinkled with pink and yellow flowers spanned the ground between the marble temple and the mountains. Mitch laughed and pointed behind her, directing her to take in the full wonderment of their surroundings. A huge crystal castle sat atop a multi-hued crystal mountain reflecting shades of blue, purple, orange, and yellow.

Rachel's mind tried to wrap around the incredible spectacle. Her heart pounded as she stood in the glory of this fantasy world.

"This is only part of what this world offers," Mitch said.

Rachel was stunned. It was hard to articulate what she was feeling. She looked at Mitch, smiling, and hugged him again.

"Thank God I found you! I thought you were lost forever."

"I'm glad you found me, too. It will be even better now that we can experience this place together," said Mitch. Rachel was thankful that he held her shoulders; it helped steady her.

"This place is amazing, but we need to get back to Mom. She barely speaks since you went missing."

"I'm not sure we can get back. To be honest, I haven't even tried. There is no place I'd rather be than here. There is no need for money, no stress, no expectation. And look at this place!" His hand swept around, calling attention to the environment like a spokes model demonstrating a product. "There is nothing back home that compares to what I've seen here. Ancient temples, iridescent waterfalls, shimmering mountain ranges, an amethyst cave... even a face carved in stone that has gold light flowing from its mouth like a fountain."

Rachel realized others were watching their interaction. There were 20 people with glassy eyes, smiling and gesturing for her to come deeper into this unknown realm. Some of them had crystal arms that matched the landscape; others had started the transformation with only their fingers resembling clear quartz. She recognized a few of them from her research on those that disappeared down Dark Hollow Road.

"How long have these people been here?"

"Some have been here as long as 100 years! Seems like there is no limit to lifespan on this side of the portal," Mitch said.

His enthusiasm was disconcerting to Rachel. "Can we take a walk and talk about this privately?"

"Sure."

Mitch put a hand to her upper back and guided her toward a cobblestone path. Pink clouds drifted in the pale sky over the deep blue mountains.

"Mitch, something doesn't feel right here. It's beautiful and Walt Disney would probably be inspired to create a section of the park called Crystal Realm or something like that, but it is strange that these people are growing crystals on their bodies. My guess is that the ones who have been here the longest have the most crystal body parts, right?"

"Yeah, that seems about right. But who cares if you get to live in Utopia forever?"

They walked past an opalescent crystal just under six feet tall. Rachel looked toward the bottom to see what held it in place and saw the only thing that remained of the crystal's original form – the tips of toes protruding from a pair of sandals. Rachel's hand flew to her chest, trying to calm her racing heart. For a moment, she could not breathe. Oblivious, Mitch continued his list of the benefits of living there, until Rachel punched him in the shoulder and made him look at the creepy image.

He shrugged his shoulders. "That happens sometimes, mostly when people lose their desire to be here. Then the process speeds up."

"Doesn't that worry you? What if you decide you want to leave at some point?"

"I can't imagine that. Back home is dull compared to this. I have nothing to go back to."

Rachel shook her head, astonished that her formerly level-headed brother had fallen for this weird and dangerous realm. Her mind raced to find the magic words to convince him to find a way out. She sought to calm herself before she said the wrong thing.

"What about Mom and me? We love you."

"But you're here now!" Mitch said, smiling.

Rachel's jaw clenched as she wondered how their roles had been reversed and she had become the sensible one.

"And we have arrived at a special place," Mitch announced.

Rachel looked up to see a tall gate glowing white hinged onto a gray stone wall. Bearded faces wearing jeweled headdresses stared down at them with an air of superiority. The gate opened slowly. Through the opening, Rachel saw a blue and purple stone building with columns lining the entrance. From the doorway a bright white light radiated. She felt pulled toward it, but fought against its beckoning. For the first time in this realm, she was afraid. Her body shook, and she grabbed hold of Mitch's arm for support.

He loosened her grip and told her not to worry. His words did not console her, and she turned to flee. Mitch grabbed her arm and shook his head no. The light was growing brighter and from the beam emerged an illuminated being holding a staff. It looked like an angel, yet Rachel's gut tightened at the sight of it. She tried to pull free from Mitch, but he dragged her toward the creature.

"This is Azziz," Mitch said, as though introducing an old friend. "Azziz, my sister, Rachel."

Azziz turned, shimmering brilliantly, and glided silently into the building. Mitch pushed Rachel through the doorway and got behind her, blocking her exit. The gate began to close behind them.

"Come on, Mitch! Let's get out of here! I have a really bad feeling about this!" Rachel pleaded to deaf ears.

"Relax," he ordered.

The chamber they entered was lined with crystal sentinels, former humans now charged with upholding the edicts of Azziz. Rachel wept at the sight of these lost souls, hopelessness compounded by her brother's devotion to this entity. Rachel grew weak from struggling, any effort to escape blocked by her brother. Azziz spoke to their minds, voicelessly, telepathically. It felt sharp inside her head—probing spikes attempting to eclipse her will and manipulate her desires. Mitch released her arm, knowing she was now under the control of Azziz.

I am here to save you from yourself. Love me more than you love yourself and everything is yours for the taking. Your destiny is here, your happiness is here. There is no world except this one.

Rachel's knees weakened under the pressure of Azziz's will. She collapsed to the marble floor, her head bowed, her eyes closed. His thoughts pushed hers aside, reaching to fill her brain, seeking to remove her from herself. Struggling against the painful invasion, Rachel conjured thoughts of home, her mother, her friends, and her goals. Never before had any of it seemed as important as they did in that moment.

Azziz brightened against her attempts to darken his power over her, filling her mind with blinding light that pressed against the inside of her eyes. Rachel squeezed her eyes tighter and fought to sustain images of her house, her school, and the life she envisioned for herself. In her wildest dreams, she never aspired to become a crystal statue under the control of a deceptively angelic demon. Her refusal to be controlled came forth in a powerful scream. She could no longer feel her body; neck pulsing and nostrils flaring, she clamped her hands over her ears as she screamed no at her attacker.

Mitch jumped back, surprised by the sudden shriek that split the air and shook him out of the stupor Azziz had lulled him into. Confused as though just awakening from a deep sleep, he looked around to see Rachel on her knees defying Azziz with sound and will. On the platform in front of him, Mitch saw Azziz's light flickering as the two battled for control. Conflicted, he stood on the sidelines, hands covering his ears to reduce the sound of Rachel's rebellion, unsure of what to do. This was the first apostle he brought before Azziz, and was embarrassed at his sister's behavior. She was making him look bad in front of his master.

Mitch cautiously shifted his gaze to Azziz, his stomach rolling, and his hands trembling as he watched the transformation from a creature of light to a deadly entity of darkness. Spots of black had begun bursting through the white aura, the mouth downturned with pointed teeth protruding from blood-red lips. Mitch wanted to hide, to run. He should have listened to Rachel, but now it was too late. Sweat made his clothes stick to his body, the sounds building to crescendo as the beast fought against this seemingly lesser creature.

Rachel's face was twisted, eyebrows clenched in concentration, her hands in tight fists of revolt, straining against the power of the beast. She began running a mental list of things she was grateful for, feeling the fury directed at her from this monster. Recognizing that Azziz hated the energy of gratitude gave her the ammunition she needed to go against him. His formerly solid light turning to formidable darkness now wavered before Rachel. She needed to finish him soon; her strength was diminishing, her mind and will growing tired.

Mitch saw her falter, her pain like a slap in the face, pulling him back to himself. Rachel strained to turn her head toward him, trying to hold on to her psychic fortress while simultaneously sending him their special signal. He felt it as a bright ping in the center of his forehead, indicating that she was in trouble and needed his help. They devised this method as children, Mitch ever the supreme protector of his little sister. Wherever Rachel was, she could contact him and he would follow the beacon to wherever she was.

This time it was different. The pinpoint of brightness contained information beyond a cry for help. It urged him to focus on their love for each other and how much they cared for one another. His mind filled with happy memories of board games and roasting marshmallows in the fireplace, of snow angels and swinging on their play set out back, of family pets and building forts. This was the most important fortress they had ever built together, one that could protect them from the monster that threatened both their lives. Their eyes met and the thread of their bond connected.

A lifetime of joy and love was too much for Azziz. It pricked holes in his appearance, shifting and cracking his power until he writhed in agony. Overcome by the coordinated efforts of Rachel and Mitch, Azziz shrieked in anger and burst in a monumental blaze, exploding the crystal soldiers and blowing a hole in the roof of his temple. Mitch and Rachel blocked the burst with heads down, forearms thrown over their heads and across their eyes. The blast was momentarily violent, followed by a strange calm previously unknown to the crystal realm.

Rachel slowly lowered her hands and looked at Mitch, who gave her two thumbs up.

"Let's get out of here!" said Mitch.

Rachel was definitely ready and followed Mitch out of the temple. The gate was now gray and bent, no longer serving to lock unwilling souls into the ruins of the temple. They stepped over the twisted metal and onto the cobblestone path. The rest of the environment remained intact, its magic unconnected to the vibrations of Azziz. The siblings walked in silence back to the area dominated by the crystal castle.

The population awaited their return, their faces no longer smiling. A few of them looked much older than when Rachel first arrived. The rest seemed confused. The energy had changed, and they seemed unsure of their place in this realm. Rachel had expected the magic of the place to be destroyed along with Azziz, yet the extraordinary landscape remained. It was still not where she wanted to live.

"I vote we look for the portal that takes us home," said Rachel.

"I'm not sure if I'll be able to get back, since I've been here for quite a while now."

"It's only been about four weeks. What's the worst that could happen?"

"Anyone else want to get out of here?" Rachel asked the group.

They looked at each other and then at her, dazed, not comprehending what she was asking. Rachel tried again.

"Anyone want to go home?"

It seemed like the word home struck a chord, as several of them were nodding yes and others had their hands clasped in prayer and their lips pressed together. All were staring at Rachel with expectation. She started walking in the direction of the creek, the others parading behind her.

Along the way, she picked a crystal flower as a gift to her mother, and put it in her pocket. Wondering if the flower, along with the people that had crystallized, would make it through the portal, she searched the landscape for the swirling vortex of color. Her eyes landed on a ripple in the air, blues and purples emerging in wavelets. As she had done on the other side, she chose a weighty stone and tossed it through. It slipped in just as it had done in the woods.

"We'll go through first, and then you guys come through behind us," Rachel instructed, hoping they would actually do so. It would be wonderful for them to be reunited with their families.

"You'll be back," one of the realm's longtime residents said to Rachel. "We are without a leader."

She looked at him, her brow furrowed. She opened her mouth to reply and decided it was not worth the effort. If he was interested in staying, so be it. She was out of here. Reaching behind her for Mitch, they clasped hands and silently agreed they were ready to step through. Taking several steps closer, Rachel was gently sucked into the portal with Mitch behind her. Moving forward, she was anxious to reach the other side. This was not the relaxing journey she experienced the first time; Rachel felt agitated and uncertain she would reach the other side. Mitch felt her tension and squeezed her hand, reassuring her that he was still there.

Slowly propelled by the cosmic goo, their bodies supported and weightless, the density of the substance beginning to thin, Rachel's hopes grew. A few more moments and they were spat out the other side with a blurp, the vortex closing behind them. Mitch looked around him, his eyes twinkling at the sight of the deep green woods surrounding them.

"Your car is over there," Rachel pointed, still feeling the tug of the portal, to the vine covered vehicle. "We should really cover up the portal. All this time, everyone thought it was the road that was cursed. This thing lures you in. It's impossible to fight it."

Rachel watched Mitch walk over to his Mustang, pulling vines off and hoping it would start. "Man, it'll be great to drive this again."

Rachel did not respond. He turned toward her, but she was gone.

~ ~ ~

Rachel popped out the other side of the portal, back to the crystal realm, horrified to see the residents looking at her, smiling and nodding.

"What the hell..." Rachel protested.

"You had to come back," the crystal-armed man explained. "You defeated Azziz, so you are now the Guardian of the Realm."

"But I don't want to be..."

"Your transformation has already begun. We will rebuild your temple and ensure your comfort, Master. Welcome home."

The Restaurant

"How did you find this place, Marilyn?"

"Online, of course, where I find everything else."

"It seems a bit out of the way. What do they have?"

"The description said 'a unique blend of exotic and intoxicating ingredients masterfully woven together.' Now if that doesn't whet your taste buds, nothing will."

"That could be anything! And possibly something gross, like beef tongue in a stew of caviar and swamp eel!"

"Arthur, don't be ridiculous! Let's check it out. If we don't like the menu, we'll leave and go someplace else. Make a right up here."

Arthur turned the wheel, frowning. The car was pointing down a dark alleyway.

"Are you sure this is right?"

She checked the printout one more time. "It's what the Mapquest directions say," she confirmed.

Arthur tentatively maneuvered the car down the center of the narrow alley between the oxblood red brick walls spattered with white spray-paint letters warning them to "go back" and giving them a pause with "trouble ahead" written in a hurried hand. He looked over at Marilyn, whose eyes were fixed straight ahead looking for a sign for the restaurant.

"There it is!" she pointed as she spotted the worn, hand-painted sign. "Garden of the Gods."

"It looks kind of run down to..." Arthur's sentence was cut off by a brilliant flash of light that temporarily blinded them both.

Marilyn's arms went up to defend against the brightness and Arthur ducked and cupped one hand over his eyes as though it was merely sunlight penetrating the windshield. The flash dissipated as quickly as it had come, leaving the car perfectly parked in front of a revitalized building with windows that glowed blue. Arthur and Marilyn sat stunned looking around at the clean brick walls, the expansiveness of the formerly narrow alleyway, and the beckoning signage of Garden of the Gods.

"What the hell was that?" asked Arthur.

"Got me," Marilyn said. She was as puzzled as he was. "At least it doesn't look like a derelict neighborhood anymore."

"And how do you suppose that happened?"

"I have no idea."

"It's like we went through some kind of portal and came out into another dimension where everything is new."

Steve had seen enough sci-fi movies to know that whenever there was interdimensional travel, the journey was punctuated with a flash of light and the surroundings were similar yet changed in some way. He was reluctant to get out of the car, not knowing what kind of alternate-dimension creatures could be awaiting their succulent selves. Maybe the restaurant was just a front to feed their carnivorous pets a snack of human flesh.

A knock on the window jarred him from his ruminations. A willowy body bent to allow his eldritch face to appear at the passenger side window. His rust-colored eyes were too large for his long, pale face and slender nose. Lips that were as blanched as the rest of his skin tone grinned to expose stained teeth. Marilyn leaned away from the stranger's gaze and toward the safety of Arthur's arms.

"You have 8 pm reservations, yes?" said the man at the window.

"Yes," said Arthur.

"You're right on time. Allow me to get the door for you," he said, trying the handle on the door.

"Well? Should I unlock the door, dear? This is the restaurant you wanted to try. Are we going in?"

Marilyn was undecided.

"It's an experience you won't want to miss," encouraged the man.

"We don't have a lot of choice, Marilyn. We're not in Kansas anymore."

Arthur popped the electronic door lock and the man lifted the handle, opened the door, and extended his hand to help Marilyn from the vehicle. This guy was so long and lanky he imagined his nickname must be "Slim."

"Go ahead," Arthur said, pushing her shoulder only slightly.

Marilyn extended her hand into the large, sweaty palm of the out-of-proportion man and allowed herself to step out onto the alien pavement. Arthur opened the driver's side door and got out of the car. He looked up and down the wide street. No one else was out on this balmy September evening. The moon was five days from the full Harvest Moon and large enough to brighten the piece of sky at the end of the alleyway.

"By the way, sir, my name is Rot, Cornelius Rot," said the man Arthur formerly thought of as Slim. "You may call me Cornelius."

"Will do, Cornelius," said Arthur, wondering if it was just a weird coincidence that the moment he had attached a name to this guy, he had been corrected.

Returning his attention to Marilyn, he saw the look of trepidation on her face as Cornelius Rot led her into the entrance of the restaurant and gave her an encouraging nod. This evening was turning out to be much more interesting than he had anticipated.

Rot looked over his shoulder as Arthur followed close behind Marilyn.

As they entered, the heavenly aroma of garlic, wine, and other herbs wafted from the kitchen. The raised panel mahogany walls were well polished and created a luxurious feel in the small space. Five round tables were comfortably placed about the main dining room, some with two chairs and some with four. Green cloths woven with gold thread were set with fine china sporting a Grecian border and sparkling cut crystal goblets. The room seemed to have a glow to it not attributable to the décor.

Cornelius turned sideways and extended his hand in introduction. "Gossamer will seat you," he said.

Before them stood a man wearing a shimmering white suit and a gentle smile. His eyes gleamed as he looked at his guests.

They followed him in silence. Patrons, talking in low murmurs, filled all of the seats, except at the table where they led Arthur and Marilyn. The waiter pulled out a chair for Marilyn while Arthur seated himself.

"Looks like you're full tonight," Arthur commented.

"All anticipated guests have arrived," replied Gossamer as he handed them the menu.

The six-by-nine-inch menu was bound in brown leather with gilded letters. A single sheet of what looked like parchment was affixed to each inner panel. Arthur and Marilyn glanced over the menu and then wide-eyed at each other. The menu read:

Seafood:
Caramelized Sea Serpent on bed of seaweed w/Saffron Beurre Blanc Sauce
Filet of Mermaid w/hearty Bordelaise Sauce (wine)
Reptile:
Slow roasted Five Spice rubbed Dragon Tongue w/horseradish sauce
Poultry:
Griffin Chaucer Style (hunter sauce w/wild mushrooms)
Stuffed, roasted Phoenix w/cranberry and clove Dressing
Meat:
Centaur thigh au vin (wine sauce)
Medallions of Minotaur Marsala
Center Cut Unicorn Steak w/grated horn and au poivre (peppercorn) sauce

Gossamer poured water into the crystal goblets. It had a golden glow. Arthur started laughing.

"Is this for real?" Arthur asked Gossamer.

"Oh, very real, sir. I only regret that we are out of the Mythical Salamander Soufflé. It's quite popular among those seeking to renew their strength and bolster their courage," Gossamer replied.

"None of these creatures exist in the real world. They're mythological," argued Arthur.

"It depends on what you consider 'the real world.' They do exist in the ether realm, where you are now, in great numbers actually," said Gossamer matter-of-factly. "That makes them mystical rather than mythological. They have been glimpsed by occult adepts that crossed into the ether realm by astral travel and brought news of them back to the physical plane."

Marilyn looked up at him in a panic.

"You mean we've crossed into a place that is only accessible through the practice of magic?" said Marilyn. She wasn't sure whether to be excited or frightened out of her mind.

Smiling, Arthur looked over the menu again. He wanted to believe this crazy story, and from all indications like the bright light and changed environment, there was no reason to believe he was still in the world familiar to him.

"So what do you recommend? Arthur asked Gossamer.

"Are you kidding me? You're actually going to eat these creatures?" Marilyn said, alarmed by Arthur's willingness to partake of these mystical beings.

Gossamer interjected with assurance. "Madam, only those who are ready to transform find our quaint dining establishment."

"But it was on the Internet and listed as a location in Mapquest!" she objected.

"Visible only to those who are meant to be here," clarified Gossamer.

"How do we decide what to order?" Arthur ignored Marilyn's protest and continued to consider his options.

"Each entrée is expertly prepared by our chef, Jasmine Nyte. Her methods bring out both the flavor and the orphic properties of the selection," explained Gossamer.

"Orphic properties?" Marilyn was still not convinced.

"Yes, the metaphysical attributes associated with each creature. I've heard it succinctly stated as 'you are what you eat.'" Gossamer smiled at Arthur. "To answer your question, sir, any of your choices will be quite delectable and pleasing to the palate, so my recommendation would coincide with the type of powers you are seeking to acquire."

Eyebrows went up on both Arthur and Marilyn at this statement. Marilyn's interest was piqued.

"Powers?" Marilyn wanted to make sure she understood exactly what he meant by that.

"The magical powers that each mystical creature holds is transferred to whoever eats their meat," explained Gossamer. "It is a blend of your own nature and that of the creature, so results are unpredictable."

Arthur's right eyebrow lifted and the opposite corner of his mouth turned up in a half smile. Marilyn recognized this expression as Arthur's reaction to an opportunity to be taken advantage of. She'd seen it many times before, each time with mixed results.

"I've always wanted super powers. Okay, I'm game," said Arthur. "Dragons have always been a favorite fantasy creature of mine, so I'll take the Dragon's Tongue." He chuckled as he realized his choice was close to the beef tongue in caviar he joked about earlier.

"Fine choice, sir. The dragon has many desirable powers, with the tongue legendary for the ability to influence any man or woman to your way of thinking. And for you, Madam?"

"I'm not sure I'm that hungry."

"Come on. When will we get another chance like this?" Arthur instigated.

Marilyn's thoughts turned to the hand-painted unicorns that adorned her room as a child. She always loved their beauty and their magic. Guilt welled up at the idea of eating one of her treasured memories. Was it possible to experience their magic by eating one? She wet her lips and, with a pained look, said, "I'll have the Unicorn, please."

Gossamer nodded and collected their menus. "A fine choice. Unicorn is quite a delicacy. To eat one is to take on the ability to sense evil and heal wounds."

Arthur took a sip of golden water, feeling his lips tingle as he watched the waiter walk away. He dabbed his mouth with a napkin.

A tiny woman with long wavy black hair and pointed ears brought a basket of oat bread and a plate of olive oil for dipping. The sleeves of her garment sparkled with every movement, despite the absence of sequins.

"Bread and olive oil assist in absorbing the magical properties of the food," she said, her eyes twinkled with the same flash as her dress. She flitted from table to table, bringing other guests the same bread and oil. Her fairy-like movements reminded Marilyn of Tinker Bell, her feet barely touching the ground as she worked.

Arthur and Marilyn split the loaf and dunked it in the oil. Warmth radiated through their bodies with the first bite. Ecstasy overtook them and they moaned with delight.

"If the bread is this good, I can't wait to taste the main course!" Arthur said between chews. The sommelier appeared at their table, holding a bottle of pinot noir, pouring it into their wine glasses.

"This wine was specially selected to enhance your dining experience and is included with your meal," he said.

Arthur raised his glass to Marilyn, approving her choice of restaurants, and took a drink of the nectar. Marilyn returned the toast, feeling flushed from the savory liquid.

Gossamer returned holding their entrees.

"The Dragon Tongue for Monsieur and the Unicorn for Mademoiselle," he said, putting their plates in front of them.

In addition to the entrees, each plate was piled with kernels of corn mixed with pomegranate seeds. Arthur's Dragon Tongue and Marilyn's Unicorn Steak were drizzled with their accompanying sauces in the shape of some sort of symbol. Delicate lines joined three small, medium, and large circles filled with complex patterns. The chef must be an artist as well, thought Marilyn.

Gossamer enlightened them on their side dish. "Corn to sacrifice the old life and pomegranate to assist in death of the old and allow you to be reborn anew. Enjoy!"

Arthur and Marilyn clinked glasses to the sentiment. Gossamer bowed and walked away. They, along with the other diners, dug into their meals, each bite more scrumptious than the next. Conversation in the room was replaced with moans of ecstasy as patrons chewed and drank, mouths full and heads nodding in approval. The wine steward kept their glasses full throughout the meal.

Finished, Arthur wiped his mouth and sat back, hand on his stomach. Marilyn took her last bite and sighed with satisfaction. They felt full and euphoric. Gossamer was there to clear their plates.

"May I interest you in dessert or coffee?"

"I couldn't eat another bite," said Marilyn, Arthur shaking his head in agreement.

Arthur looked around the dining room. The other diners looked as though they had finished their meals, as well. Gossamer produced their check inserted in a leather binder and held with red ribbons. The total came to $175.

"Not bad for endless wine and mystical meat," marveled Arthur. He handed over his credit card.

"If you'd be so kind as to fill out our comment card with your address and date of birth, we will send you special coupons for a free meal on your birthday," said Gossamer.

Arthur willingly completed all the information on the card and checked the highest rating of "extraordinary."

Cornelius had their car ready outside. "I trust you had a pleasant evening," he said.

"Definitely did. We'll be sure to come back!" said Arthur.

"I'm sure you will, sir," Cornelius affirmed.

The now familiar flash of light momentarily blinded them once again and they found themselves in the dim alleyway headed to the main drag taking them in the direction of home.

~ ~ ~

Marilyn primped in front of the bathroom mirror while Arthur finished dressing in the bedroom. He wore his best suit in preparation for the big meeting he had with an advertising client he had been trying to land for quite some time. While his reputation was confirmed by his many sales awards as an account executive for one of the up-and-coming advertising agencies in the area, he felt especially confident this morning, ready to take on any challenge. There was no objection he could not overcome; there was no concern he could not alleviate. Arthur straightened his tie and did a fist pump to psych himself up.

He popped into the bathroom to kiss Marilyn goodbye. She grabbed his shoulders and pulled him close, landing a big smooch on his lips.

"You'll be great, Honey!" she encouraged him. "No one could say no to you the way you look. I can feel the power!" She smiled with admiration, looking forward to celebratory sex that inevitably followed after he landed an account.

"Thanks, Babe! See you tonight."

Tweezers in hand, Marilyn turned back to the mirror to tackle an incredibly stubborn stray, gray hair that had grown dead center between her eyebrows. Her attempts to yank it met with severe resistance and quite a bit of pain. The repeated attempts to remove it had resulted in red irritation around the area. She decided to give it a rest to avoid further skin damage. Foundation covered the redness, and she figured the hair was not that noticeable.

Arthur arrived at the office, confidence high, energy blazing as he attracted the attention of all he passed on his way to his office. This was going to be the day he conquered the elusive client. His prowess at influencing would become legendary after this meeting. Those walking by his glass-walled office gave him a nod in greeting, and his smiled beamed back at them. They knew he was their ace-in-the-hole.

His secretary, Janice, peeked her head in and said, "Mr. Ortho is waiting for you in the conference room." She smiled and gave him a thumbs up.

Arthur straightened his tie, buttoned his jacket, and strode confidently out of his office and down the hall. He greeted Charles Ortho with a Cheshire Cat grin and an outstretched hand. "Good morning, Charles!"

"Good morning, Arthur. I'm looking forward to seeing what you have for me today, although I'm not convinced that this will be any better than the last bunch of ideas."

"This campaign is going to knock your socks off! You'll be ready to write a check by the time you finish watching the pitch." Arthur assured him.

"I certainly hope so," said Arthur's boss, Adam Carter, entering the room with an authoritative air. He smiled and shook Ortho's hand.

He shook Adam's hand and frowned. "We'll see," Charles Ortho was skeptical. The last few ad campaigns were cliché and did not fit the brand image of his company. He was not sure why he was giving this guy another shot at getting his business. There was something in Arthur's voice when they made the appointment for this meeting that convinced him to play along. He sat down and crossed his arms.

As Adam made light conversation with Charles, Arthur rolled down the screen and pulled up the presentation on his laptop. The projector affixed to the ceiling sprang to life, lighting up the panel. Adam got up and flicked off the overhead lights. A few clicks of the keyboard, and the first slide came up.

From his seat at the head of the table, Adam watched for signs that the client was either engaged or ready to walk. Arthur had not been able to win over this client during past pitches, and this was their last shot at signing him. To his surprise, Charles Ortho watched mesmerized as Arthur took him step-by-step through his ideas, ideal target audience, and rationale for the approach.

The client uncrossed his arms and opened his posture to what he was seeing, absorbing every nuance. Adam, too, was drawn into the presentation, silently applauding Arthur's ability to convince their client to embrace his approach, but he felt confused. It was similar to Arthur's last idea, with only minor changes; yet this time, the idea seemed plausible and the perfect campaign to launch Ortho's new product line. Each word, each gesture built one upon the other, inspiring them both, exciting the mind and the senses to see Arthur's vision for the future. Arthur had convinced them both to move forward with his proposal.

Arthur wrapped up with the request for his commitment today and a deposit to get started on making this multi-million dollar campaign come to life. He shut off the projector.

Charles Ortho looked stunned, and Arthur waited for the rejection once again. Adam held his breath.

"Okay," Charles Ortho said, a sly smile creeping onto his face.

"Okay?" Arthur echoed.

"Yes, let's get this thing off the ground. I'll have my assistant send over a deposit. I'm pleasantly surprised. Good job, Arthur!" He stood up and, smiling broadly, shook Arthur's hand. Adam let out his breath and nodded his approval.

"Great! Let me walk you to the door." Arthur was excited, but wanted to come across as though he knew it all along, maintaining balance between his delight and utter surprise at Ortho's reaction. He glanced over at his boss, who gave him a subtle thumbs-up.

Marilyn sat at her cluttered desk at the travel agency, staring at her computer screen and fingering the stiff gray hair that seemed to be getting larger as the day progressed. It was less pliable and seemed thicker. Her lunchtime trip to the beauty salon down the street for an eyebrow waxing had proved unsuccessful in uprooting the stubborn sprout.

The woman performing the service said she had never seen anything like it. Even cutting it proved impossible. Oddly, the girl had cut her forefinger earlier, and when she absentmindedly used it to test the texture of the gray hair, she felt a tingling. When she looked at her finger, the cut was gone. She rationalized that maybe it wasn't as deep as she had originally thought.

Now, several hours later, Marilyn looked into the pocket mirror she carried in her purse, to see the hair prominently protruding from between her bangs out as far as her eyelashes. She bit her lower lip at the sight. The others in her office kept snatching glimpses of her, frowning and quickly looking away. She could not walk around like this!

The bell over the door tinkled and a man walked into the room.

"Can I help you?" asked Carole Sloan, an agent sitting at the desk closest to the door.

"I'd like to get some information on cruises. It's a surprise for my wife. Something in the next couple of months leaving from New York City."

"Sure, I can help you with that!" Carole brightened at the prospect of a sale.

Marilyn watched them chatting and exchanging information. She had a bad feeling about this guy. He was not interested in taking his wife on vacation; he was interested in pushing her overboard while they were at sea. The thought made her jump a little, and she pulled back. What had made her think that? She tuned in to the man once again, and in her mind's eye saw him shoving his wife over the side of the ship and grinning and waving goodbye as he watched her scream and claw at the air, no one hearing her over the roar of the ship's engines. She turned away from him to cut the vision.

How awful! Marilyn was certain that he would follow through with his plan, and there was nothing she could do about it.

~ ~ ~

Arthur rushed through the door, grinning from ear to ear. "Marilyn!" he called from the doorway. "I did it!"

The house was quiet. The normal clattering of pots and utensils signaling that dinner was being prepared was conspicuously absent. Arthur walked through the house trying to pinpoint Marilyn. Her car was in the driveway. Where could she be? "Marilyn?"

The master bedroom was at the back of the house. The door was open, and he could see Marilyn's legs stretched out on their bed. "You okay?" His news taking a backseat to whatever would make his Energizer Bunny wife lay down so early in the evening. As he rounded the doorway, he gasped, getting full view of her body and head. A twisted, whitish-gray horn about five inches long stuck out from between her eyebrows. Tears ran from the corners of her eyes.

Arthur's hand covered his mouth, shocked at the spectacle that was his wife. "What... what..."

"Happened? What does it look like? I have a horn sticking out of my head! Just like the kind unicorns have!"

"You don't really think that..."

"That the meal we ate at the restaurant had anything to do with it? What else could it be?" she said, throwing up her hand and accidentally hitting the horn. She sobbed harder.

Arthur sat gingerly on the bed, putting his hand on her leg, seeking to comfort her. "Maybe it can be surgically removed."

"I couldn't get it out even when it was just a hair! It's like it's part of me; attached to my skull!"

Arthur's tongue touched his upper lip in thought. He saw a shift in how Marilyn looked at him.

"What the hell is that?" she exclaimed.

"What the hell is what?" he said, alarmed.

"Your tongue!" she cried.

He jumped up, ran to the mirror and stuck out his tongue. It was much longer than normal and split down the middle. He stared, horrified, as his tongue lengthened to impossible proportions. He was able to lick his eyebrows.

~ ~ ~

The full transformation happened quickly after that, their forms changing into the mystical creatures they had eaten. Unable to leave their home, Marilyn the Unicorn and Arthur the Dragon spent several days foraging for food in their kitchen. With their hands and feet morphed into hoofs and claws, they were unable to cook or take care of themselves in the usual way. They looked at each other with dread and foreboding at their predicament.

One night, they heard the front door open and footsteps cross the entry foyer. Gossamer and Cornelius Rot entered the room where the former Marilyn and Arthur had once shared a bed. The two men produced a glimmering net, seemingly spun of silver, and expertly wielded it, capturing the Unicorn and the Dragon. The net prevented them from fighting their captors, and they were helplessly dragged from their home under the light of the full Harvest Moon and into the back of a livestock transport, where a Mermaid, a Phoenix, a Minotaur, and a Griffin waited. They were all encased in the same silver netting, looking at each other with the saddest eyes imaginable.

The back of the trailer was closed, and they heard Gossamer and Cornelius Rot talking as they walked toward the truck's cab.

"Good thing the transformations are complete. Looks like a good crop this time," said Rot.

"We'll have enough meat, fish, and poultry for the world leaders and business magnates who have already made reservations for our first seating in October," said Gossamer.

"I love how you tell the story of getting the mystical creatures from the ether realm. It's all I can do not to laugh every time I hear it," Rot chuckled.

"Chef Jasmine will be pleased with the size of these catches. She included a special ingredient in the oat bread that plumped them up nicely," Gossamer reveled in his employer's skill.

"Chef Nyte let me assist during the last meal preparation and taught me some of the magic she uses. The symbols she draws on the entrees, with the catalyst of the golden water fosters the transformations. I'll have to wait

until the next Harvest Moon for another chance to work alongside her."
Gossamer shook his head.

"Yeah, without the symbols and the golden water, the high-paying
customers simply get the powers of these creatures without the unpleasant
side effects," said Cornelius Rot knowingly. "It's worked that way for centuries."

The livestock transport pulled away, heading toward the portal and The
Garden of the Gods, where Chef Jasmine Nyte awaited the delivery.

Wrong Directions

Hatred dripped from her fingers and into the small electronic pod she assembled. This custom-made gift would be his reward for repaying her devotion with deception. She squinted through the magnification lens at the tiny components. It was her masterpiece, although no award for innovation would be bestowed upon her; no one could know. Motivated to invent by his cheating ways, she had created a sensitive electronic instrument imbedded with deadly energy not of this world that would literally drive him to the Pit of Hell.

Nova Blackmon was the best electrical engineer at Technodyn Electronics. Trained at MIT, she was a prodigy, graduating with a doctorate at the age of 21. At five feet ten inches, her statuesque appearance, cascading chestnut hair, slender waist, and large bosoms caught the attention of the men she worked with. She could have had an intimate relationship with any of the scientists at Technodyn, but she was in love with one man: her husband, Ian Blackmon.

Sparks flew between them from the moment they were introduced at the international electronics conference in London. Nova was charmed by his British accent and pleased that he was three inches taller than she was; Ian was impressed by Nova's intelligence and excited by her physique. A mutual friend introduced them after Ian's presentation on wireless computer technology applications. It was refreshing to meet someone closely matched to Nova's intellect and socially adept as well.

That was then. Of late, the charm had not only worn off, but had been scraped, gouged, and beaten off of their relationship. In one brief moment, a seemingly idyllic marriage collapsed in a sonic blast of horror, disgust, and resentment. Nova's inner radar guided her to sit across from Ian's office one day at lunchtime. She watched as the two of them emerged from the brick building, Ian's arm cast around his blonde secretary, Samantha Porter. It explained all the late nights at the office. The bastard had told Nova that Samantha held no interest for him, and squirmed throughout her interrogation. Nova continued her surveillance long enough to see the secretary open her sultry mouth to receive Ian's lying tongue. Their actions were too grotesque, too familiar with each other, for Nova to believe that this was their first time together.

It was then that Nova pledged devotion to something other than Ian and her work; she was determined to learn the dark side of the occult and use it to reduce his hard-on to a quivering pile of flaccid flesh. Academically inclined and driven by anger, Nova was able to master the Dark Arts within months. Her diligence was fueled by images taken of Ian and the blonde with a camera she devised that fit into the face of the watch she had given him for his birthday last year. Her intuition had told her that something was amiss, and she had learned to trust her instincts.

With all that she learned during her studies in sorcery, she found that she was particularly adept at conjuring demons. First calling upon the lesser demons to make sure her containment spells were effective in controlling the nasty little creatures, she graduated to increasingly more powerful entities, calling them and banishing them until she found Balthazar.

Its revolting appearance, brownish green, and dripping with slime and muck from the bowels of its home allowed it to slide smoothly into its new abode, disguised to behave as a high-tech navigation device complete with audio functionality. Balthazar's voice was scratchy and deep, so Nova trained it to speak in an appealing female voice she knew would engage Ian. As Ian suckled on his secretary, so Balthazar would feed on the hate that Nova poured into every component of her project.

As the sorceress that brought Balthazar forth, she had a special telepathic connection with the demon that she could engage whenever she liked. She would always be able to locate him and, hence, her device of revenge.

Nova was pleased that she was able to complete the project in time for their eighth wedding anniversary and proudly presented it to Ian over a candlelight dinner she prepared at home. The entire evening was a surprise for him, since he had completely forgotten the happy occasion.

"A GPS! I've been wanting one of these! Thanks, Nova." Ian kept his eyes on the new toy.

Nova kept her eyes on Ian's face. He never made eye contact and had been avoiding it all evening. "You're welcome," she said with a smirk.

"It's just that I've been so busy at work, and you know that I rely on you to remember important dates."

The excuses just kept coming, so she knew that he was not prepared to reciprocate. Not that he could have come up with a gift the equivalent of the present she bestowed upon him.

"Don't worry about it. I know how distracted you've been lately." She maintained eye contact as she slowly sipped her red wine, picturing him covered in blood, the eyes that would not look at her pulled from their sockets and laying on his cheeks. She grinned at him and he gave a tentative smile back.

"I'll make it up to you," he promised, clueless as to how he would even begin to do that.

He wondered if Samantha would be this understanding if he had forgotten something important to her. For a moment, Ian remembered why he had fallen in love with Nova. Then her accusing eyes made him shrink back to thoughts of his mistress.

Samantha did not have the intelligence or confidence that Nova possessed, so she was easier to manipulate. Being with her was easier because she expected less from him. Nova was his intellectual equal and many times exceeded his capacity for innovation and cognitive creativity. It was intimidating and made him feel less of a man. Samantha made him feel superior being easily impressed by his accomplishments.

Ian forced himself to make love to Nova as part of their anniversary celebration. He felt that she was allowing it out of courtesy, for she did not show the hunger for him that she once had. His sense of inadequacy grew in her presence, once again justifying his relationship with Samantha. It would be a relief to go away for a romantic weekend with Samantha. He would tell Nova that he was invited to speak at a conference this weekend and that he would be home Sunday night.

~ ~ ~

Nova grinned and waved as Ian pulled out of the driveway late Friday afternoon. She had seen him plug in the address for his weekend tryst into the GPS. It was hard to believe that he thought she was so naïve as to be completely unaware of his activities. With Balthazar on board, Ian's wild weekend would end sooner than expected.

Ian was relieved to get out of range of Nova's intense gaze. She seemed to accept his tale without question; yet her eyes told him that she knew better. For a moment, he considered canceling his plans and pulling back into the driveway, but images of intense physical intimacy with Samantha pushed him to continue on his way to her house. Once Samantha was in the car, he would feel better.

Samantha's smile radiated sunshine into the vehicle and over his worried face. The short cotton dress she was wearing exposed the smooth skin of her thighs. Ian placed his hand on her upper thigh just under the skirt line. Samantha covered his hand with hers, encouraging him to go higher if he wanted. Normally he would have, but Ian could not shake the sense that Nova was somehow with him.

He set the GPS to lead them to their secret place and pulled away from the curb. A silky female voice told Ian to make a left at the next corner. Samantha commented that if she did not know better, she would be jealous of the sultry sounding woman emanating from the gadget on his dashboard. Ian forced a smile, thinking of Nova's gift causing Samantha to be jealous.

The GPS worked perfectly, guiding them accurately toward their destination in the mountains. Ian knew they were getting close as the trees grew dense and the road became serpentine. A steep cliff followed the road to their right. The guardrail protecting cars from going over the edge seemed insufficient, given the sharp drop. Samantha's moans at Ian's probing distracted him. With the road dangerously winding, he pulled his finger out from between Samantha's legs, to her dismay. Their groping would have to wait until they reached their destination.

The velvet female voice instructed Ian to make a sharp right in 400 feet. The instructions made no sense, for the screen did not show a street on the right. His forefinger covered in Samantha's juices poked at the reset button of the GPS, expecting revised instructions. The voice came again, instructing him to make the turn. Ian felt his foot press down on the accelerator. He tried to lift it, but it continued to press harder until the car reached 50 mph, much too fast to navigate the curving road safely.

Balthazar held Ian's hands frozen to the steering wheel, the unnatural grip turning his knuckles white. Samantha's screaming provided an annoying backdrop to his panicked thoughts. The voice came through the speaker, telling him to turn in 100 feet. The silken voice was gone, replaced by a gravely male voice that commanded Ian to make the turn.

He fought against the pressure of the invisible force that made him begin turning the wheel to the right, inching the car closer to the edge of the cliff. Ian wished Samantha would shut up. He could not concentrate. He felt her grab the wheel to help turn them away from the open air waiting for them on the other side of the guardrail. It made no difference.

The harsh voice began laughing; the evil sound sent waves of horror through Ian. He had no time to say goodbye to Samantha before the unseen force jerked the wheel to the right, sending the SUV crashing through the guardrail and sailing over the cliff onto the rocks below.

~ ~ ~

The police found the bodies splayed on the rocks, the bones of the once beautiful faces of Ian and Samantha smashed, giving them the look of melting flesh. Samantha's skirt revealed scraped and bloody thighs, red chunks of flesh revolting rather than enticing.

Sergeant Matt Bell was first on the scene, the winding road heading toward the Palace Resort, his regular patrol. Matt figured the bodies had been laying there since the night before. He discovered them around 6 am. The coroner confirmed Matt's educated guess.

He could see that the blood covering the rocks near the bodies had begun to turn dark, indicating freshness of the cadavers. With no sound and no movement coming from below and the way the bodies were twisted and partially impaled on the jutting rocks, Matt knew there was nothing the Emergency Medical Technicians would be able to do for them.

It was odd the way that the guardrail had seemed to explode outward into the canyon. He would expect it to bend outward, but an entire section was missing, jagged edges remaining as markers where the safeguard had once held.

The bodies were thrown through the windshield, seatbelts ripped as though made of crepe paper. It took hours to open the crushed doors to gain access. Matt found identification for both victims inside the vehicle. With the drop being at least 200 feet, a helicopter winch lowered the crew down and lifted the bodies out of the ravine. Closer inspection of the bodies revealed the woman's lack of undergarments; over the years, he had seen accidents caused by sexual escapades while driving. Mangled skulls had spewed pieces of brain across the stone and were now baking on the sun-heated rock. The crew kept scavengers from feasting until they analyzed the scene.

Matt called the home of Ian Blackmon at approximately 11 am. A woman answered the phone and indicated that she was the wife of Ian Blackmon. That complicated matters, for Matt never liked giving news of a death, let alone the death of a man found lying on a bed of stone with another woman.

He informed Mrs. Blackmon of her husband's demise as gently as possible, indicating a motor vehicle accident as the cause and letting her know that they found him at the bottom of a ravine in the mountains. Matt did not indicate a female companion found at the scene. It reminded him of his ex-wife's illicit affair with their next door neighbor. When he came home early and found them entangled on the green and tan striped background of the living room sofa. Overwhelmed, Matt thought of pulling his gun, but chose to keep his hands balled in tight fists and clenched his teeth. His eyes threw daggers of devastation stabbing Elaine in the heart. He could see that she felt his pain. He was reluctant to deliver this delicate news to a widow.

He let the widow know where she could identify the body and told her how sorry he was to call with such disturbing news.

As he hung up, it struck him as odd that the widow did not sound surprised at the news. She had sounded amazingly accepting of the situation, saying that Ian was heading to a resort to give a presentation and that he was never one to be especially careful.

They hauled the SUV up the side of the cliff. Once at the top, the sergeant took the opportunity to search the vehicle for indications of possible alcohol involvement, such as an open bottle, but found nothing.

Battered beyond repair, the vehicle's windows were smashed, the steering wheel was bent, and the seat belts were shredded. That was something Sergeant Bell had never seen before. Apparently, the victims were wearing their seatbelts; yet due to the impact or maybe the result of metal from the vehicle's frame cutting into them, they had released the passengers, flinging them violently onto the rocks. There must be a logical explanation, but none that Matt came up with could account for the odd way the seat belts were shredded.

The navigation device formerly attached to the now smashed and broken windshield was on the floor in perfect condition. Matt would have expected it to be demolished in the crash, but along with everything else that was unusual about this case, he was not completely surprised to find yet another anomaly. He lifted it out of the vehicle and bagged it along with Mr. Blackmon's suitcase to return to the widow. A final search turned up nothing more of value to salvage from the wreckage, so Matt released it to the tow truck to take to the impound yard. The technicians there would check to see if the breaks had given out or if there had been any other mechanical malfunction in the vehicle that precipitated the accident.

~ ~ ~

At the door of the Blackmon residence, Sergeant Matt Bell presented with a sorrowful face as he delivered the surviving possessions of Nova's husband. She asked him if he would like to come in, and he accepted. Sitting in the living room of the comfortable contemporary home, Nova let him know that she had been down to the morgue to identify the remains and that it had in fact been her husband.

She also had the opportunity to identify the person with him as his secretary. While she had been unaware that she would be accompanying Ian to the presentation, she told the officer that it could have been the case that he needed her there to assist him in gathering information about the attendees to the presentation or some other similar business. Matt felt that Nova was being exceedingly understanding about the presence of another woman at the scene, more so than he would have been.

Nova displayed sadness as she told Sergeant Bell of her theory and did her best to convince him that she did not suspect her husband of cheating on her. The way Sergeant Bell pressed his lips together and lowered his eyes as she offered an explanation for Samantha's presence in the car, she could tell that the officer was trying to hide his suspicion that Ian had been heading to the mountain resort to screw his attractive secretary.

As the door closed behind him, Sergeant Matt Bell's intuition bristled at the casual manner in which Mrs. Blackmon had received the news that her husband was in the company of his secretary heading to a resort known for clandestine trysts. The staff's discretion and the hotel's remote location made it perfect for secret romantic rendezvous.

~ ~ ~

On the other side of the door, Nova cradled the cursed GPS in its plastic blanket and smiled at the incredible efficiency of her creation. Balthazar did better than expected, killing both Ian and Samantha in one eloquent step. Sergeant Bell did not believe she was so naïve as to be unaware of her husband's infidelity, but no matter. They could search the vehicle, look at its mechanical stability, or ask questions of everyone connected to Ian, Samantha, or herself, all they wanted – they would find nothing that linked her to their deaths.

Those who knew her could swear that she would never air dirty laundry in public or speak ill of the dead, hence her reluctance to point the finger and accuse her husband of cheating on her with his secretary. It was all neat and clean and, judging by the condition of her supernatural instrument of death, indestructible as well.

Telepathically checking in with Balthazar, he reported feeling at home in the electronics of the cozy casing and enjoyed the work assigned him.

The perfect condition of the GPS lent itself to becoming a gift for those in need. Nova no longer needed it; it satisfied its original purpose. Her search for a new owner would commence tomorrow.

~ ~ ~

At the bookstore down the street from her home, Nova planted herself with a cup of tea at a table in middle of the store's café. This vantage point was ideal for eavesdropping on those seated at tables around her. She listened for conversations about cheating husbands as she quietly sipped her drink, waiting for her prey, like a spider in a web. Really though, she rationalized, her intentions were honorable. After all, she was poised to help an innocent wife end the suffering bestowed upon her by a wicked spouse. It was not really murder.

Nova was almost to the bottom of her beverage when in walked two women in their thirties. They sat nearby, far enough away that they thought they could talk in private. Nova had excellent hearing, especially when boosted by a concealed listening device implanted in her ear.

"I don't want to be suspicious, but I can't help it," said the blonde.

"What makes you think he's cheating on you?" asked her red-headed friend.

"Late nights at work, doesn't look at me when I talk to him, no desire to make love, and longer hours on the computer." The blonde-haired woman took a sip of her coffee.

"Those are certainly some of the signs. What would you do if you found out he was cheating on you?"

"I'd kill him," she said, her fist clenched on the table.

"Rita, you don't mean that!"

"Why not? He humiliated me and exposed me to God-only-knows what kind of diseases!"

"I guess, but a divorce would certainly suffice," offered her friend.

"Wiping him off the face of the earth sounds better to me. Besides, that way I'd get the house, the life insurance, and be able to start with a clean slate." She smiled at the thought of revenge and financial security. "I know it's only a pipe dream; there's no way I could actually kill him myself. I'm not wired for violence and I wouldn't want to get caught." She looked down into her coffee cup, tears welling in her eyes.

"There's got to be another way to resolve this. Try to find out if your worries are justified, and then take appropriate action once you know for sure."

Rita nodded in agreement without looking up at her friend.

Nova watched them get up and walk toward the exit. She stood as well and saw them on the other side of the glass, finishing their conversation. They hugged and turned to walk their separate ways. This provided her the opportunity she needed to speak to the blonde, Rita, about her options.

Before she got her attention, Nova activated a glamour spell that hid her identity. Rita would see her as a fellow blonde with a large nose and tanned skin.

"Pardon me," said Nova.

Rita turned. "Can I help you?"

"No, but I can help you. I couldn't help overhearing you talking to your friend."

The woman looked puzzled, wondering how Nova could have heard them from such a distance away. She decided not to ask and simply waited for Nova to explain what she meant.

"It's devastating to find out your husband is cheating on you," Nova empathized.

"Are you his mistress?" said Rita, feeling a lump in her throat.

"Certainly not! I'm someone who has experienced the pain in my relationship that you're going through now."

"So what happened? Are you still with your husband?"

"He died. They found his car at the bottom of a ravine, his body lifeless and battered... along with that of his mistress."

The woman's mouth fell open, her eyes wide. She realized how she must look and closed her jaw. "Did you..." she stammered, unable to finish her sentence, afraid of hearing the reply.

"I was nowhere near the vehicle when it crashed, if that's what you mean. I gave him an anniversary gift and then saw him off." Nova smiled.

"A gift?"

"This." Nova held up the GPS. "He always wanted one, so I made sure he had the perfect instrument. It was custom-designed for him. Amazing that it survived such a violent crash."

"Amazing," Rita whispered.

"Now that my husband no longer needs it, I thought I'd be generous and pass it on to someone who it could serve. You, that is. Your husband could greatly benefit from having this navigation device in his vehicle."

Rita squinted at Nova, surmising the consequences of giving the GPS as a gift to her husband.

"What if I'm wrong about him cheating?"

"Nothing will happen to you... or to him, if he's being a good boy. But if he's not, this gadget is sensitive to that kind of behavior and will act accordingly. The wishes you made when talking to your friend will become reality. I believe you said you'd like to 'wipe him off the face of the earth.'"

"You're saying that you'll give this to me to take care of my problem? And that there's nothing else I need to do?"

"That's correct," Nova smiled and nodded.

Rita hesitated. She no longer saw the cars whizzing by or heard the construction project around the corner. There was only an angelic hand holding the answer to her problem. She reached out her hand to accept the cursed item.

"Just give it to him as a gift and let the machine do the rest."

Rita nodded in understanding, shoved the GPS in her purse, and quickly walked away from Nova, realizing she never asked for her name nor did the woman ask for hers and that she could not remember what the woman looked like. It was probably better that way. She turned to steal one last look at her blonde benefactor, but all she saw was a woman with Chestnut hair looking in a shop window.

~ ~ ~

Rita sat across from her husband, Brandon, in the small dining area of the apartment they rented. She did not need much in the way of décor and never thought to complain about the size of their residence, but a larger dwelling with more closet space would be nice. They might have been able to afford something larger if Brandon had not spent so much money on his bimbo. She watched him chew the steak she had cooked him, hoping it was his last meal.

It had been two months since the guardian angel had given her the solution to her problem. Waiting tortured her, knowing he continued his fling, following him to make sure her next move was justified. Seeing them together fueled her hatred and strengthened her desire to destroy him.

"Aren't you hungry?" asked Brandon, not really caring.

"My stomach is a little upset," she said, the thought of going through with her plan making her stomach roil.

"Since it's my birthday, I thought we'd go out after we finish eating."

"I'm not feeling very well, but if you want to go out, I understand," all too well, she thought. "But first..." Rita reached under the table and pulled out a wrapped package, "... happy birthday!"

Brandon smiled at the purple-and-white striped wrapping paper and fluffy gold bow. He ripped into it.

"A GPS! Mine hasn't been working right. This is great. Thanks, Babe." He blew her a kiss.

Don't call me, Babe! She screamed inside her head. All that came out was "You're welcome. Happy birthday."

"I can't wait to try it out. Are you sure you're not up for going someplace? We could catch a movie or go out for dessert someplace."

"I'm sure. Sorry. I know you want to celebrate. Call one of your buddies. I'm sure they'd be happy to help you continue the party." Rita knew exactly which buddy he would call.

Brandon wiped the corners of his mouth, came around to Rita's side of the table, and kissed her forehead. "Okay, then. Feel better!" He took his new GPS, put on his coat, and left without calling anyone.

Rita watched his every movement, considering for a nanosecond taking back the deadly gift. Brandon's choice not to call a friend from the house strengthened her resolve and she bid farewell to Brandon for the last time.

Balthazar rode in his new victim's pocket, waiting for the opportunity to take action.

~ ~ ~

Matt was puzzled at what would make a man drive straight into a stone wall, completely missing the tunnel opening. From the accordion shape of the Chevy Malibu, he must have been going 75 MPH. Both airbags had deployed and then burst under the pressure, the steering wheel then driven into the man's chest. His wallet indicated his name was Brandon Guess. It was anyone's guess as to what went through his mind in the last moments of his life. Matt shook his head at his own bad pun.

The windshield was smashed, the cracked safety glass partially intact, with the rubber sticker of the GPS bracket still affixed. The GPS itself rested comfortably in the bloody lap of Kelli Butler, her head now one with the dashboard.

~ ~ ~

Rita Guess was appropriately saddened as the police officer handed her Brandon's wallet and the surviving GPS; tears flowed easily at the news of Brandon and Kelli's deaths. She cried in relief, in despair, and in true sorrow that Brandon had pushed her to take action. If only she had been wrong, he would still be alive. Plans for her new home and a fresh start replaced remorse. The job done, she could pass on the GPS to another deserving woman.

~ ~ ~

Sergeant Bell was confused by the rash of fatal car crashes in the area. These were not the type where teenagers, having tested their limits of alcohol consumption, smashed their cars into trees or into another vehicle; this was different. In each case, a married man with a female passenger that was not his wife, were found dead in or around a vehicle that was destroyed beyond expectation in ways that forensics could not adequately explain. The men were running their cars into telephone poles, into lakes, over cliffs and bridges, and into oncoming traffic. Regardless of the extensive damage to the vehicle, no matter how mangled the windshield or auto body, the GPS survived, whole and functional and covered with blood. There had to be a connection between the cases. Each victim seemed to be an adulterer and the GPS came through unscathed, ultimately returned to the widow of the deceased husband. The widows had seemed sad, yet behaved as though the death was expected.

Matt Bell wondered how he would have felt if his cheating ex-wife had ended up dead after he found out about her affair. Would he have a similar reaction as the widows whose husbands were turning up dead? On some level, he could understand their reaction if they were previously aware of the spouse's betrayal. But if they had no idea, the reaction should have been shock and grief. None of these women seemed shocked at neither the death nor the fact that her husband's body was accompanied by the body of an attractive woman. Was it possible that the widows were somehow involved? Could they have planned the untimely demise of their cheating spouses?

Matt was not an expert in electronic gizmos, but all of the retrieved GPSs looked suspiciously alike. He had compared various makes and models, none of them looking similar to the GPS found at the crash sites. How could the same GPS show up at each crash site? Even if the wives were in on it, they had no prior connection to each other, so how did they share the same GPS?

~ ~ ~

Jennifer Brown was the latest scorned wife to acquire the cursed GPS. It was bestowed upon her by a woman she met in the supermarket. Jennifer had run into a neighbor with whom she discussed the suspicious behavior of her husband Carl. He left work and said he was spending time with his friends. His friends called the house, looking for him, and jokingly accused Jennifer of keeping Carl from them. Most had not seen him for weeks. She suspected he was having an affair, yet could not imagine with whom. Carl seemed devoted to her; they told each other the truth as far as she knew, but this situation made her wonder what he was hiding.

The conversation finished, Jennifer continued on with her shopping and was approached by a strange woman professing to be the solution to her dilemma. The idea of killing Carl made her heart hurt more than the thought of him enjoying time with another woman. She found herself accepting the gift and watching the woman walk away. Carl would be surprised to receive an unexpected present.

Carl was excited that Jennifer thought to give him such a great gift and for no particular reason. Unknown to her, he had taken a second job that required him to make deliveries in many unfamiliar areas. The GPS would come in handy. He felt badly for not telling her about the job; Carl did not like hiding things from his wife. All would be forgiven when he presented her with two tickets for the ten-day Mediterranean cruise she always dreamed of. Taking on the additional work was the only way he could swing it financially in time for her birthday next week. Then he could quit the job and once again enjoy quiet evenings at home with his beloved wife.

He left shortly after dinner, telling Jennifer he was meeting some friends at the sports bar to watch the game. He detested the lies and looked forward to coming clean. Carl gave her a warm, loving kiss on the mouth, hugged her, and left with the gadget that would make his deliveries go much faster. He affixed the GPS to his windshield and plugged in the addresses scheduled for deliveries that evening. The velvety smooth voice came through the GPS guiding him to turn left and go north on Route 165. Carl willingly followed the directions.

He had about eight miles to go before the next turn. The GPS spoke to him, counting down the miles before the next turn. With each vocal intrusion, the voice became deeper, darker, and more menacing. Maybe the battery was running low or there was some faulty wiring. He gave the unit a gentle slap to try to get it to behave, instead eliciting a piercing tone that made him swerve into the oncoming lane.

Sergeant Matt Bell was driving south on Route 165, heading home after a long day and wishing he had someone waiting for him at home, someone he could trust. With all of the cheating husbands he was seeing lately, his ex had been damned lucky to have him. That was one thing she never had to worry about with him. A swerving car coming onto his side of the road shook him from his ruminations. The driver tried to gain control of the vehicle, but it continued to head toward Matt. He pulled over to the shoulder, tires partly on grass to avoid colliding with the Saturn. As it passed him, he saw the panic on the driver's face, hands gripping the wheel and struggling to maneuver the car into his own lane. Matt made a sharp U-turn and followed the car, hoping to intervene before it was too late. He had had enough bloody wrecks to last him a lifetime.

Carl battled against the vehicle, which now seemed to have a mind of its own. The voice of the GPS laughed and growled, providing a hideous backdrop to a terrifying situation. Up ahead, Carl spotted a runaway truck ramp and focused on directing the vehicle toward it. His body was drenched in sweat, chest tight, and mind praying to God that he be saved. As Carl invoked God, the GPS made a gurgling sound and the light on the screen went dark. The wheel was his once again, and he pointed the car toward the truck ramp, slowly depressing the breaks to come to a full stop.

Matt pulled in right behind him and jumped out of his car, leaving the door open behind him. He ran up to Carl's vehicle. Carl's head rested on his hands, which had loosened their grip but not their hold on the wheel, breathing as though he had just run a marathon.

"Are you okay?" Matt shouted, banging on the driver's side window.

Carl leaned back and rolled down the window with his left hand, his right one clutching his chest.

"What happened?" Matt pressed.

Carl just shook his head, still trying to catch his breath. Matt's eyes wandered past Carl and to the windshield, where the dreaded mechanism gripped the glass.

"Where did you get that GPS?" asked Matt.

"My... wife," Carl said between gasps.

There was no evidentiary support to substantiate that Carl's wife had tried to murder him with the electronic device, but Matt would make sure it was never passed on to another woman. With all of the death and destruction he had seen over the last few months, he was glad that he never acted on his impulse to shoot his ex-wife and her lover. It was too tempting for scorned women to take the easy way out, not having to get their hands dirty using the unit of revenge. It was time to eliminate this option as recourse for those hurt souls that simply wanted the pain and embarrassment to stop.

He had Carl unlock the passenger side door, where he slid into the seat and dislodged the GPS from its bracket. Matt laid the contraption onto the ground, stood over it, and dropped a large rock onto its face. The unit stayed intact.

"Hey, that was a gift…"

"Trust me, you don't want it. Get another one at Radio Shack."

Matt had never been a churchgoing person, nor did he actively pray, but something came through him, guiding him to call upon God for help. He picked up the rock and holding it over the damned thing he said, "God help me destroy this evil," and dropped the rock, smashing the GPS casing to pieces, its guts scattering across the ground. Matt kicked the bits of metal around, making sure they could not find each other ever again.

"You'll be okay now. Have a peaceful evening." And life, Matt thought.

Carl decided to head home, curl up with Jennifer, and empty himself of his secret. Matt headed home, too, satisfied he had ended the parade of mangled bodies associated with the GPS.

A black, rectangular chip lay on the ground, vibrating with Balthazar's eagerness to meet his next victim. In her contemporary haven, Nova prepared dinner, chopping celery and red peppers for a salad. Her demon's energy came at her like a blow, forcing the knife to leap from the vegetables and sink into her left index finger, blood marinating the green and red pieces of food on the cutting board. Balthazar smelled the blood and knew his master had received his distress signal.

~ ~ ~

About the Author

Diane Wing is a multi-published author of dark fantasy fiction and enlightening non-fiction. She has a Master's degree in clinical psychology and years of study and experience in the realms of the occult, metaphysics, and Eastern philosophy. She grew up on *Night Gallery*, *Dark Shadows*, and *Tales from the Darkside*, and the supernatural has always been a natural part of her life. She is the founder of the mystery school, Wing Academy of Unfoldment, and host of Wing Academy Radio.

Find out more at DianeWing.com.

Diane would love to get your feedback on *Trips to the Edge*, please visit **http://tinyurl.com/tripsedge** and scroll down to "Write a customer review".

www.ingramcontent.com/pod-product-compliance
Lightning Source LLC
Chambersburg PA
CBHW020143150626
46552CB00021B/1603

* 9 7 8 1 6 1 5 9 9 2 6 2 1 *